Alien Invasion!

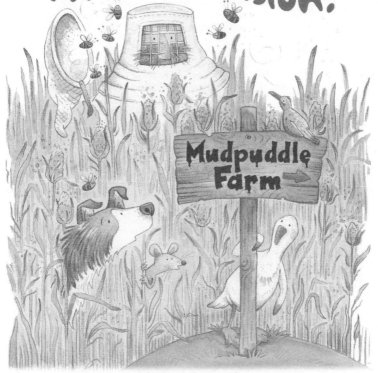

Mudpuddle
Farm

michael morpurgo

Interior illustrations by Shoo Rayner

Cover illustrations by Cecilia Johannson

HarperCollins *Children's Books*

Martians at Mudpuddle Farm first published in Hardback by
A&C Black (Publishers) Limited 1994
First published in paperback by Collins, a division of HarperCollins, 1995

Mums the Word first published in Hardback by
A&C Black (Publishers) Limited 1995
First published in paperback by Collins, a division of HarperCollins, 1996

This bind-up edition first published by HarperCollins *Children's Books* 2008

This edition produced for The Book People Ltd,
Hall Wood Avenue, Haydock, St Helens, WA11 9UL

HarperCollins *Children's Books* is a division of
HarperCollins*Publishers* Ltd
77-85 Fulham Palace Road, Hammersmith, London W6 8JB

The HarperCollins *Children's Books* website address is
www.harpercollinschildrensbooks.co.uk

1

ISBN 978-0-00-783527-0

Printed and bound in England by
Clays Ltd, St Ives plc

Mixed Sources
Product group from well-managed
forests and other controlled sources
www.fsc.org Cert no. SW-COC-1806
© 1996 Forest Stewardship Council

FSC is a non-profit international organisation established to promote the
responsible management of the world's forests. Products carrying the FSC
label are independently certified to assure consumers that they come
from forests that are managed to meet the social, economic and
ecological needs of present and future generations.

Find out more about HarperCollins and the environment at
www.harpercollins.co.uk/green

Contents

Chapter One

There was once a family of all sorts of animals that lived in the farmyard behind the tumble-down barn on Mudpuddle Farm.

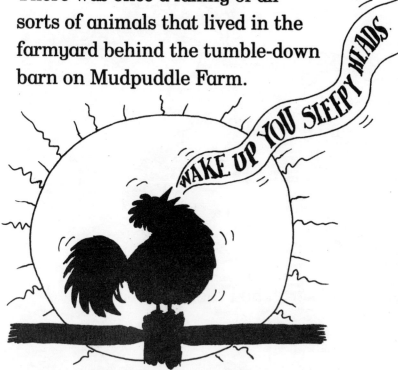

At first light every morning Frederick, the flame-feathered cockerel, lifted his eyes to the sun and crowed and crowed until the light came on in old Farmer Rafferty's bedroom window.

One by one the animals crept out
into the dawn and stretched

and yawned

YAWNNNNNNNNN

and scratched themselves.

But no one ever spoke a word – not until after breakfast.

7

Early one morning old Farmer Rafferty looked out of his window. The corn was waving yellow in the sun. The stream ran clear and silver under the bridge, and the air was humming with summer.

The bees will be out flying today, and that means honey. And honey means money, and I need to buy a new tractor. The old one won't start in the mornings like it should. Get busy bees. Buzz my beauties, buzz!

Chapter Two

Deep in the beehive at the bottom of the apple orchard, Little Bee was getting ready for his first solo flight.

Now remember, load up your pollen in the clover field, and then come straight home. And don't get lost. Good luck.

And off flew Little Bee out into the
wide blue sky. Round and round he
flew, looking for the clover field, but
he couldn't find it anywhere.

So he buzzed down towards the old
tractor where Mossop, the cat with
the one and single eye, was trying
hard not to wake up.

11

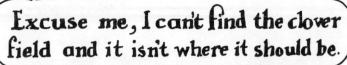

Excuse me, I can't find the clover field and it isn't where it should be.

Mossop opened his eye.

Left at the pond.

Right at the bottom of the field.

Then left again at the blackberry hedge.

Then he went back to sleep again.

The trouble was that Little Bee
didn't know his right from his left
or his left from his right.

Round and round he flew looking for the clover field, round and round till he began to feel giddy

Little Bee felt a great yawn coming on. He looked down for somewhere soft to sleep and then he saw the tractor with the old cat still asleep on the seat.

His tail looks nice and soft and warm. He won't mind, he won't even know I'm there.

And he was quite right about that. Mossop never even felt Little Bee land on his tail. He was too busy dreaming. So Little Bee and Mossop snoozed together in the sun and the hours passed.

Chapter Three

Back in the beehive, Queen Bee
was getting worried. Little Bee had
been gone for hours now and
something had to be done.
She called all her bees together.

Right, forget pollen-gathering,
forget honey-making. Little
Bee is lost and we've got to
find him before dark else he'll
get cold and die. Follow me.

Ah-ha!
Once more
unto the
breach!

Old Farmer Rafferty was milking Aunty Grace, the dreamy-eyed brown cow, when he heard the bees coming. 'There they go,' he chortled over his milk pail.

And then he began to sing as he
often did when he was happy.
He sang in a crusty, croaky kind of
a voice, and he made it up as he
went along.

Out in the clover field Diana the
silly sheep

was rolling on her back

to scratch her itches

when she saw a great swarm of bees
coming straight towards her.

She struggled to her feet and ran off towards the pond as fast as her legs could carry her. No one was at all surprised when she jumped right in. That's what she always did when there were bees about.

As usual it was Jigger, the almost always sensible sheep dog, who had to pull her out.

'And some mothers do have them,' thought Albertine from her island in the pond.

said
Upside
and Down.

So the two white ducks that no one could tell apart upside-downed themselves in the pond and stayed there all day long.

And sure enough, the sky above them suddenly darkened and the humming became a droning and the droning became a roaring.

DON'T MOVE!

But no one could move anyway. They were all too terrified, except Albertine of course.

'Albertine,' said Captain without moving his lips. 'What are we going to do?'

Chapter Four

Albertine thought her deep goosey thoughts for a moment. Then she said, 'Just follow me'. And she swam across the pond, waddled through the open gate and out into the cornfield beyond.

All the animals followed because they knew that Albertine was the most intelligent goose that ever lived. If anyone knew what to do, she would. They reached the middle of the cornfield and looked up. The bees were still following them.

Albertine began to run
round in a great big circle.

All the animals did the same, running round and round

And above them the bees all flew round and round and round.

'I wish,' said Aunty Grace,

I wish someone would tell me why we're doing this. The bees aren't going away and I'm feeling giddy.

Me too dear!

said Primrose.

'Good,' said Albertine.

If you're feeling giddy, then the bees are feeling giddy.

She's so logical!

So round and round they all ran until suddenly the buzzing stopped. When they looked up the bees had all buzzed off, just as Albertine had said they would.

Chapter Five

The bees were flying home over the farmyard when one of them suddenly spotted Little Bee all curled up asleep on Mossop's tail. 'Follow me,' said Queen Bee and down they flew.

Yes Ma'am!

LITTLE BEE

'I got lost,' cried Little Bee.

I want to go home.

'Soon,' Queen Bee yawned.
She could hardly keep her eyes
open, she was so sleepy.

But first we'll hang about here and have a little snooze.

And so that's what they all did.
Soon there was a great ball of
snoozing bees hanging on
Mossop's tail.

MEANWHILE....

Back in the cornfield, Captain had
a worried look on his face.
'Just look what we've done to
Farmer Rafferty's corn,' he said.
'Just look.' And they looked.

They had flattened out a huge circle in the corn. Not a single solitary stalk still stood standing.

They all heard him. He was walking into the field singing his honey song.

honey, oh honey. won't you b

When Farmer Rafferty reached the middle of the cornfield, there wasn't an animal to be found. What he did find was a great circle of flattened corn.

And he began to chortle and his
eyes began to twinkle.

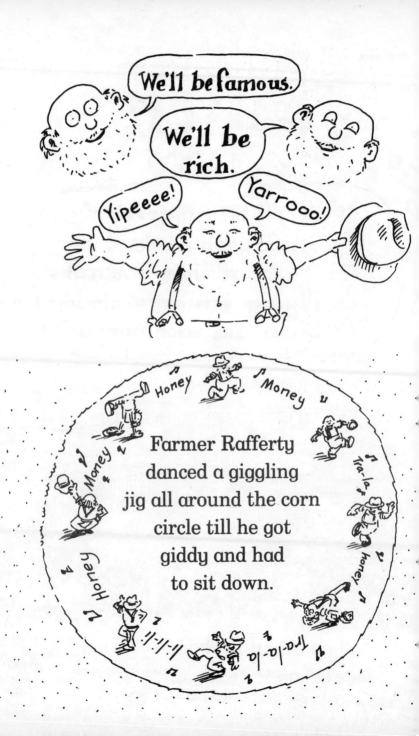

Then off he went towards the farmhouse, counting on his fingers and muttering to himself.

He didn't know it, but from behind the farmyard wall the animals were watching and listening to every word.

'What's a Martian?' Diana asked
and of course everyone looked at
Albertine.

'Well,' she said, thinking very hard
indeed, 'they walk stiffly like robots
do and they carry ray-guns like
Farmer Rafferty says.' The animals
could hardly believe it, but if
Albertine had told them then it had
to be true. After all there was
nothing Albertine didn't know.

Chapter Six

Farmer Rafferty was still counting
on his fingers when he passed by
the old tractor and noticed the ball
of bees hanging on Mossop's tail.

Oh dear me. My bees
have gone and swarmed.
Perhaps they couldn't find
the way back home. I'll
have to put them back in
their hive.

And he disappeared inside the
farmhouse.

While he was gone, the animals
crept back into the farmyard, just
in time to notice something coming
in through the farmyard gate.
It was dressed in white from
head to toe.

It wore a white helmet

and white gloves

and it walked stiffly like a robot,

and as it walked it puffed smoke
out of its ray-gun.

In its other hand it carried
a great big sack.

A Martian!

Diana cried. And she ran, they all ran. They ran until they came to the edge of the pond where they found Albertine washing herself.

'It's a Martian,' panted Jigger, the almost always sensible sheepdog.

Albertine smiled her goosey smile.

Look again.

That's not Martians, that's Old Farmer Rafferty in his bee-keeping costume. Now watch...

And they watched as old Farmer Rafferty puffed smoke around the swarm of bees.

Farmer Rafferty scooped the bees
into his sack, and off he went
singing his honey song, with Queen
Bee and Little Bee and all the
others still snoozing inside.

Chapter Seven

Later that afternoon the first cars
arrived. Before long, Front Meadow
was filled hedge to hedge with cars,
and there were people everywhere.
Mossop, who had woken up by now,
walked down the lane and met
Jigger and the others.

It says...

RAFFERTY'S CORN CIRCLE
GENUINE
<u>MARTIAN</u> <u>CORN</u> <u>CIRCLE</u>

To visit .... Two Pounds

Car Park .... Two Pounds

Martian Cream Tea ..... Two Pounds

(Honey <u>not</u> Strawberry Jam!)

'No one's going to believe a silly story like that, are they?' said Jigger; but when Albertine looked at him he wished he hadn't said it.

'I think,' said Albertine 'that we believe mostly what we want to believe.'

Chapter Eight

That afternoon Farmer Rafferty showed all the visitors round his Martian corn circle.

After that they settled down on the
front lawn to a Martian cream tea.

He told them the story of the flying
saucer and the Martians that had
landed on Mudpuddle Farm, and
they swallowed it all (the cream
teas and the story) and went
home happy.

And old Farmer Rafferty was happy
too. He'd soon have enough money
to buy his new tractor.

All red and shiny it would be, with
a proper cab on it so he could
plough his fields without getting
wet and so Mossop could sleep out
of the wind.

But Mossop was quite happy out on
the old tractor in the farmyard.
None of the animals ever told him
about the day the bees swarmed on
his tail. They thought it might give
him bad dreams, and they didn't
want that.

The night came down, the moon came up, and everyone slept on Mudpuddle Farm.

Chapter One

There was once a family of all sorts
of animals that lived in the
farmyard behind the tumbledown
barn on Mudpuddle Farm.

You are the sunshine of my life...

At
first
light every
morning
Frederick, the
flame-feathered
cockerel, lifted
his eyes to the sun
and crowed and crowed
until the light came on in old
Farmer Rafferty's bedroom window.

One . . . . by . . . . one,
the animals crept out into the dawn . . .

. . . and stretched . . .

68

. . . and yawned . . .

. . . and scratched themselves.

But no-one ever spoke a word, not until after breakfast.

One morning, Captain was crunching away at his last mouthful of breakfast hay when he noticed something was wrong.

Someone was missing. Gone!

Albertine and her little goslings were preening themselves on their island.

Upside and Down
were upside down
in the pond.

Peggoty and her little piglets,
including Pintsize, snuffled and
snorted around the dungheap.

Diana the silly sheep who couldn't
count to save her life, was counting
the clouds.

Penelope and her chicks scratched and scuffled in the orchard, never too far from Frederick.

Grace and Primrose grazed nose to nose in the meadow.

Jigger, the almost always sensible sheepdog, was chasing his tail again.

And Mossop, the cat with the one and single eye, was curled up asleep on his tractor seat as he always was.

BUT, where was Egbert the grumbly goat?

Jigger, have you seen that grumbly goat?

Nope, I'll have a look shall I?

So Jigger looked and looked.

Egbert wasn't anywhere. He'd done a bunk, buzzed off, gone walkabout.

If anyone knows where he is,
thought Jigger, Albertine will,
because Albertine always knows
everything. So Jigger ran down to
the pond.

Albertine, have you seen Egbert anywhere? He seems to have gone missing.

But Egbert did not come back. The animals searched here, there and everywhere for him.

But it was no good, he couldn't
find him anywhere. No-one could
find him.

'I can't think where he's gone,' said
Grace, the dreamy-eyed brown cow.
'Nor me,' said Primrose, who
always agreed with her.

I don't know where he's gone either.

'I know, I know,'
said Diana, the
silly sheep.

He's gone missing!

'Don't worry,' Albertine told her
little goslings.

That goat will be back, you'll see, around suppertime I should think.

she's so reassuring.

Chapter Two

Sure enough, just as Old Farmer
Rafferty was giving all the animals
their supper that evening, Egbert
wandered into the yard, grumbling
as usual.

'Egbert, where have you been?' asked Farmer Rafferty in the nasty, raspy voice he kept for special occasions.

'Worried sick we were,' said Captain, the cart-horse that everyone loved and who loved everyone.

But Egbert wouldn't say another
word about it.

Down on her island in the pond,
Albertine shook her head, smiled
her goosey smile and thought deep
goosey thoughts.

Chapter Three

It wasn't long after this that Egbert
began behaving very strangely
indeed. For one thing, he stopped
grumbling. Everyone thought he
must be sick, but he wasn't.

'Good morning,' he'd say as he passed by,

And he'd say that with the wind whistling through the farmyard and the rain thundering down on the corrugated roofs.

Then one day, Diana the silly sheep
saw something very, very strange.
She saw Egbert dancing! And he
was singing too!

la la la la la la

Of course none of the animals believed her at first, because Diana was always silly. But she told them and told them until they had to come and look.

And of course, when they saw it with their own eyes they had to believe it. Egbert was dancing in the puddles, and singing his heart out.

in the rain.... what a wonderful feeling

I'm happy again

SPLISH

SPLOOSH

SPLASH

SPLOSH

'He's really sick,'
said Jigger sadly.

'Hope it's not catching,' said
Penelope, hurrying her chicks away.

'He's gone loopy if you ask me,' said
Peggoty, keeping her distance at the
top of the dungheap.

Mossop opened his one and single
eye and shut it again.

I'm having a bad dream about a singing, dancing goat that's lost his marbles. I think he ought to see a vet.

But Grace and Primrose liked the song so much that they found a puddle of their own and joined in.

Albertine sighed and smiled secretly to herself.

'You'd never understand, Captain,'
said Albertine; and Captain felt
very stupid.

Captain couldn't understand what
Albertine was talking about, but he
didn't want to say so in case she
might think he was as stupid as he
felt he was.

Chapter Four

It was Tuesday, and Tuesday was always the day Old Farmer Rafferty went off to market.

He put on his best jacket and his best hat. Then he scooped Mossop off his tractor seat and drove to market.

Off he went, happy as a lark,
singing to himself as he always did
when he was happy though he could
never remember the words.

But Old Farmer Rafferty had
forgotten something else, too.
Something much more important
than the words. He had forgotten to
close his vegetable garden gate.

Later that morning, Egbert was feeling even hungrier than usual.

I've chewed the last of the paint off the gate. I've eaten the last of the paper sacks. I've nearly eaten my rope, but I'm still hungry.

CREAK

RUMBLE

GROAN

Then he saw Farmer Rafferty's garden gate swinging in the wind, squeaking on its hinges.

'Carrots,' he thought. 'Apples.'

No-one saw
him tippy-toeing
out of the farmyard
except Mossop, who
happened to open his one
and single eye as Egbert passed by.

My goat dream again, only now he's on his tippy-toes and ballet dancing!

And he went back to sleep to finish
his dream.

All morning long, Egbert chomped and chewed his way through Old Farmer Rafferty's carrots. No-one noticed what he was up to until after lunch.

Early in the afternoon, Peggoty was taking her piglets for a stroll. As usual Pintsize had run on ahead. That was why he reached the garden gate first. Pintsize knew, and all the animals knew, that none of them (except Mossop because he was special), was ever allowed inside Old Farmer Rafferty's vegetable garden.

So when he saw Egbert standing in the middle of the vegetable garden with a carrot in his mouth, he knew that there was going to be trouble, big trouble.

Pintsize loved it when other people
got into trouble for a change.

Peggoty could not believe her eyes.
There wasn't a single carrot left
except the one in Egbert's mouth.

The little piglets gasped. Peggoty let
out her screechiest scream and
called for help.

And all the animals came running
as fast as they could.

'Egbert!' cried Captain. 'Out of there! Out of there! If Old Farmer Rafferty catches you in his vegetable garden your goose will be cooked!' And then he thought about what he'd said.

Oh, I'm sorry Albertine.

munch munch

But Albertine just smiled.

See? I told you Captain, didn't I? Carrots.

But Captain still didn't understand.

'I'll get him out,' said Jigger, the almost always sensible sheepdog. He dashed into the garden and tried to pull Egbert out by his rope. But Egbert would not budge.

Captain came in to help as well but still Egbert dug his heels in and would not move.

Oh come on Egbert. Old farmer Rafferty will be back in a minute.

In fact, Old Farmer Rafferty was just at the end of the farm lane, talking to Farmer Farley from the next door farm. 'Goats,' Farmer Farley was saying, 'who'd have them? They go where they want, eat what they want, do as they please. Still they make you laugh don't they?' And the two of them just laughed and laughed.

Back in the farmyard, the animals all heard Farmer Rafferty coming up the lane on his tractor. He was still singing away.

'I'm off,' said Jigger.

'Me too,' said Captain.

But Albertine decided to wait.
'I think I'll just stay and see what happens,' she said.

Pintsize hid under Albertine's wings and pretended to be a gosling.

As Old Farmer Rafferty came through the garden gate, all the animals hid behind the wall and watched.

Suddenly, Old Farmer Rafferty stopped singing. With bated breath, the animals waited for him to shout in his nasty, raspy voice. But he didn't.

All he said was:

You silly old goat, eating all my lovely carrots. Still, I expect you need them more than I do.

And Farmer Rafferty laughed and laughed. He picked up Egbert's rope and led him out into the orchard.

You have all the apples you can find my dear. You'll get fat, but that doesn't matter does it? You eat as much as you like.

The animals could not believe their ears. They could not understand it at all. But Albertine could. She smiled her goosey smile and waddled off back to her pond. Then she climbed up on to her island and tucked her head under her wing and slept. There were four little goslings under her wing that night, and one of them had trotters.

Chapter Five

It turned out just as Old Farmer
Rafferty had said. Egbert did get
fat, very fat. It wasn't surprising –
he did nothing but eat all day long.

He ate anything and everything –

Captain's
best hay,

Jigger's
biscuits,

Peggoty's
pigmeal,

Penelope's
corn,

Diana's
sheepnuts,

and Old Farmer Rafferty's socks off
the washing line.

He even ate the sack that Mossop
used for his bed on the tractor seat.
'I'm not dreaming this,' said
Mossop, yawning hugely. 'That goat
is eating my bed.' Mossop was not
at all happy about that.

Right, that's the last straw.
What are we going to do
about that goat?

No-one knew what to do, but they all knew something had to be done. So they went off to ask Albertine. If anyone knew what to do she would.

But Albertine was being very secretive. 'Mum's the word,' she said inscrutably, and she would say no more.

Mum's the word.

what's inscrutable?

It means mysteriously unfathomable.

Oh!

'Well I think that goat needs to lose some weight,' said Grace, the dreamy-eyed brown cow.

And I agree. He's almost as fat as we are, and we are Cows. We're supposed to be fat.

But how do you get thin if you're fat?

'Jogging,' said Jigger.

So five times a day all the animals, except Albertine who would sing along quite happily, and dance in any puddles he could find. Afterwards they did their aerobics, and all the while Egbert thought it was all very silly, jogged round Front Meadow.

Ridiculous!

'I'm singing in the sun, singing in the sun,' (or rain, depending on the weather). He didn't seem to mind the exercise at all, just so long as he could carry on eating afterwards.

And that's just what he did. He got fatter,

and fatter,

and fatter.

And to everyone's amazement, he stopped grumbling completely. The animals could not believe it.

'I'm just the happiest, luckiest goat
in the whole wide world,' he said
jumping into another puddle.

'What's he got to be so happy
about?' said Jigger. 'What's
happened to him?' And he went to
ask Albertine again.

But Albertine was keeping mum.
'Mum's the word,' she said
inscrutably, and she smiled a secret
goosey smile again.

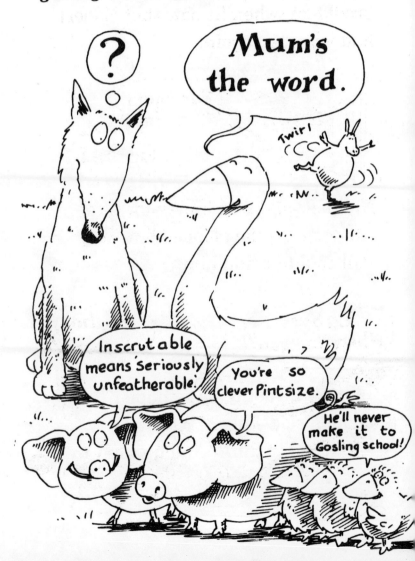

Chapter Six

Then one morning, Captain was looking out of his stable after his breakfast, when he saw that Egbert had vanished again.

Not again!

Gone!

No-one could find him anywhere. All day long they looked but they still couldn't find him.

At last they went to tell Old Farmer
Rafferty the bad news.

We've lost him again, we've lost Egbert!

But instead of saddling Captain and
going out to look for him, Old
Farmer Rafferty just leant on his
spade and laughed and laughed.

Why don't
you have a
look through
my sitting-
room window?

POW

ZIP

Jigger got there first.

'Oh yes he can,' laughed Old
Farmer Rafferty. 'He can and he
has because *he* is a *she*.
Egbert is Egberta,
and she's just had
two lovely kids.'

And they all
peered in at the
window. There was
Egberta lying out on
the sofa, a cushion under her head,
with her two little kids beside her.

That evening, Farmer Farley
brought Billy, his billygoat over to
Farmer Rafferty's to see his kids.

'It's my Egberta who's the clever one, bless her,' said Farmer Rafferty.

'I'd say they're both clever,' said Farmer Farley.

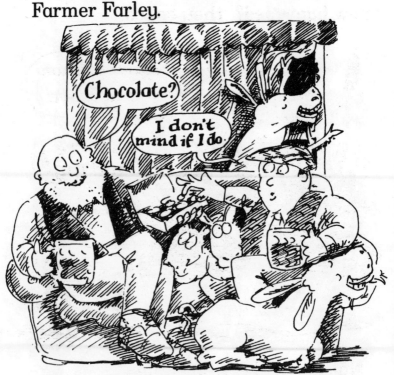

Meanwhile, Billy chewed the paint off the window and Egberta chewed the sofa, and both of them looked very happy indeed.

Chapter Seven

Out on the pond, Upside and Down came up for a breather. 'Anything new happened?' they asked.

'Not me,' Albertine smiled. 'Egberta. She's the one that's kidding. It'll be nice to have some real kids around won't it children?'

She cuddled her goslings under her wings, including the one with the trotters. 'Do you want a story to send you to sleep?' And of course they did.

The night came down, the moon came up and everyone slept on Mudpuddle Farm.